Barney

This series is for my riding friend Shelley, who cares about all animals.

STRIPES PUBLISHING
An imprint of Magi Publications
1 The Coda Centre, 189 Munster Road, London SW6 6AW

A paperback original
First published in Great Britain in 2008

Text copyright © Jenny Oldfield, 2008
Illustrations copyright © Sharon Rentta, 2008
Cover illustration copyright © Simon Mendez, 2008

ISBN: 978-1-84715-059-2

A CIP catalogue record for this book is available from the British Library.

Printed and bound in Belgium

2 4 6 8 10 9 7 5 3 1

Barney

Tina Nolan
Illustrated by Sharon Rentta

ANIMAL MAGIC
Meet the animals

Visit our website at
www.animalmagicrescue.net

Working our
magic to match
the perfect pet
with the perfect
owner!

INDIA
This playful little lady
needs a quiet, loving
home to make up for a
tough start in life.
Just adorable!

ELLIE
This lovely young dog was
locked up and left to starve.
Gentle and loving. And look
at those cute ears!

LADY
Lady loves ball games and
shiny toys. She's a wonderful
cat, happy to be with
children, looking for love.

 **HELP US**  **NEWS**  **CONTACT**

RESCUE CENTRE
in need of a home!

SOX

A sweet older cat, looking for a quiet life. Very loving, and waiting patiently for that special person.

BUDDY

Country home sought for this boisterous pup. In need of further training and strong on the lead. Perfect for a family.

SMIDGE AND SMUDGE

Owner moving away and leaving these two behind. Do you have space for them in your home?

OZZY

Poor Ozzy took a fall and broke his leg. He's mending well and looking good, don't you think?

Chapter One

"Eva, where are you?" Karl Harrison called.

Eva heard her brother's voice from way below. They'd finished collecting bedding and feed to take back for Rosie the pony and Mickey the donkey at Animal Magic, and now she lay on her back, staring up at the cobwebby rafters of Tom Ingleby's old barn. "Up here!" she replied.

Karl didn't hear her, and ran off across the farmyard still calling her name.

I love it here – I could lie here for ever!
Eva thought, as she lay amongst the sweet-smelling bales of straw, on top of a stack that almost touched the roof.

Down in the yard, her dad, Mark, chatted with the farmer.

"I owe you for six bales of straw and six of hay," Mark said, counting them off in the back of his van.

"Are you still looking for a home for that little Shetland pony?" Tom asked.

"Why – are you interested?" Mark said quickly.

"Not now that my daughter, Lizzie, is grown up and gone. I was just wondering about the pony, that's all."

"Well, we're not sure yet. Eva thinks maybe our next door neighbour will adopt Rosie in the end. But we've still got her up on the website, along with the charming Mickey!"

Tom laughed. "Yes, I can hear that donkey's bray from here – right across the fields."

"So I take it you don't want to offer him a home?" Mark grinned.

Up on top of the stack, Eva rolled on to her stomach, peered over the edge and listened.

"Not likely!" Tom replied. "Anyway, we're pretty busy at the moment, with the new house we're building for Adam. Now that we've finally got planning permission, we've made a start on the foundations. Come and have a look."

Eva watched her dad and Tom wander across the yard. She sighed and turned on to her back. It was a pity – High Trees Farm would have been the perfect place for Mickey.

She was studying the way a shaft of sunlight lit up a giant cobweb when Karl jogged back towards the barn. "Eva!" he yelled. "Where are you? I told Tom we'd sweep the yard. I'm not doing it by myself. You have to help me!"

Sighing again, Eva sat up. "OK, I'll be down in a minute," she called back.

"Now!" Karl insisted, spotting her and

holding up a large yard-brush.

Eva jumped down on to the nearest ledge, then the next, sliding from one bale to the other. "Whoo!" she cried.

"Get sweeping!" Karl said with a grin. He handed her a brush and they set to work at one end of the yard.

"This brush is heavy," Eva grunted after a few minutes.

"Moan, moan, moan..." Karl teased.

"It is! Hey, watch out – what was that?" Eva stopped work as she saw a movement in amongst a heap of straw.

"Nothing – you're imagining things," Karl muttered, moving in with his brush. "Come on, let's get this yard clear!"

There was another movement in the straw. "No, honestly, I saw something," Eva insisted. "Wait a second while I take a look."

Carefully she knelt down and lifted away a handful of straw. Sure enough, she saw a pair of bright eyes staring back at her.

"What is it?" Karl asked, coming up close behind. "A field mouse?"

"I don't know yet." Eva couldn't make it out, but she didn't want to move more straw and run the risk of seriously scaring the creature. She leaned forward and looked again.

Bright eyes and a long snout. Small furry ears. "It's a..." Sharp claws and a body covered in spikes. "...Baby hedgehog!"

"Is it lost?" Karl asked, as the hedgehog made a run for it. It scuttled out of the pile of straw, towards the barn. Then it doubled back and ran into the middle of the yard, then back again towards the barn.

"It looks like it," Eva muttered. "Where's the rest of its family, I wonder?"

"Yes, it's too little to be out by itself," Karl agreed.

They watched helplessly as the hedgehog ran here and there, finally zig-zagging back towards the barn and shuffling under a broken bale of straw.

"Poor little thing – it's scared stiff!" Eva whispered. She could just see the back end of the tiny creature and heard for the first time its high, piping cry.

"It's calling for help," Karl guessed. "Let's move away and give its mother a chance to come and find it."

Eva nodded and she and Karl retreated to their dad's van, hiding in the back and waiting for the baby hedgehog to be rescued.

After a while, their dad and Tom wandered back into the yard.

"Careful, Dad!" Eva hissed, leaning out of the back of the van. "Don't walk too near the barn. Have you seen a mother hedgehog anywhere?"

Mark shook his head. "No, but I wasn't exactly looking. Why?"

"We often get hedgehogs round here," Tom said. "Not as many as in the old days, mind you. They're a lot rarer than they used to be."

"There's a baby one in your barn right now," Karl explained. "We think it's lost."

"Ah." Eva and Karl's odd behaviour became clear to Mark. "You're hoping the mother will come back for it?"

Eva nodded. "Is it OK if I stay here and make sure it's safe?"

"Yes, if it's all right with you, Tom?" Mark took his van keys from his pocket.

Tom nodded. "Fine by me."

"I have to get back to Animal Magic with the feed for the ponies. What about you, Karl?"

"I'll come with you. I said I'd meet George and go mountain-biking."

"OK, Eva, it's down to you." Mark got into the van and Karl climbed in beside him. "You can stay. But don't get in Tom's way. And another thing – as much as you'd like to, don't get too close and start handling that young hedgehog."

Eva nodded. "I'll keep my distance, don't worry."

"Good. Because if you touch it, its mother will smell your scent when – or if – she comes back, and she'll reject it. Don't forget!"

"I promise!" Eva took the warning to heart. The last thing she wanted was for the baby to be abandoned by its mother.

Lost and alone, it would be left to blunder into ponds and barbed-wire fences, wandering aimlessly across busy roads, prey to badgers and foxes.

"Come back, Mum!" Eva muttered as she settled down outside the barn door to wait and watch. "Don't leave your baby all by itself in this big, dangerous world!"

Chapter Two

The baby hedgehog stayed half-hidden under the straw bale for a whole hour.

Eva looked at her watch, then at the tiny, prickly ball, willing the mother to appear. The sun was going down fast, lengthening the shadow cast by Tom Ingleby's barn.

"Any luck?" Tom called as he walked across the yard to his Land Rover.

Eva shook her head. "No sign of the mother so far," she replied.

She waited another half an hour without anything to report, and was about to give up when the tiny hedgehog shuffled backwards, out from under the bale. It turned and raised its snout, snuffling the air. Then it stepped timidly forward, out of the barn.

So sweet! Eva said to herself. The baby's dark eyes were set wide apart on its round face, which was covered in soft, greyish-brown fur. *It looks so funny – the way it pokes its nose forward and tilts its head back, it looks as if it needs glasses!*

Bravely now, the hedgehog ventured out into the farmyard, just as Missie, Tom's black cat, came stalking round the corner of the farmhouse.

"Uh-oh!" Eva said out loud as the hedgehog stopped, realized the danger and rolled into a tight ball.

Missie walked right up to the prickly creature. She put her nose close to the spikes, sniffing hard. The hedgehog didn't move – even when Missie stretched out a paw and tapped it gently.

Miaow! Missie discovered those spikes were super-sharp! She arched her back and hissed.

"Ouch!" Eva cringed. She watched as Missie did one full circle of the baby hedgehog then stalked off, back the way she'd come.

But the danger wasn't over for the all-alone baby. No sooner had Missie beaten a retreat than Tom's Land Rover came chugging back down the lane. Eva ran to greet him.

"Mr Ingleby, can you slow down, please? The baby hedgehog has moved and it's right in the middle of the yard where it could get run over."

"Still no sign of the mum?" Tom asked as he eased his Land Rover past the hedgehog.

Eva shook her head.

"Perhaps you should call home. Your mum and dad won't want you out after dark, remember."

Nodding, Eva took out her phone and called her mum. "Hi, Mum. Did Dad tell you about the baby hedgehog? Well, there's still no sign of the mother."

From the reception desk at Animal Magic, Heidi Harrison gave Eva her advice. "My guess is that the baby has been well and truly abandoned – probably sometime last night. That's when hedgehogs are usually out and about."

"But why would the mother do that?" Eva asked, keeping a close eye on the hedgehog, still rolled up tight in the middle of the yard.

"Who knows?" Heidi replied. "Maybe something bad happened to the mother and the other babies. Or maybe this one got separated from the rest of the family and lost its way. Hedgehogs have runs, you know. They keep to a set route each night, and if this little one has strayed a long way off the track, there's not much chance of the mother finding it again."

"So what do we do?" Eva asked after a short pause. "I can't leave it stuck in the middle of Tom's yard!"

"No, I agree." Heidi began to shut down the computer. "It looks like we'll have to bring your little baby here to the rescue centre."

"Cool!" Eva said excitedly. "What do I do?"

"You wait for me," Heidi said quickly.

"OK, and I don't touch it, like Dad said?" Eva checked.

"That's right. I'll bring a pet carrier and some cat food to tempt it in, plus thick leather gardening gloves, just in case I have to pick it up. I'll be there in ten minutes."

"Then we can drive the baby home and hand rear it! Wow, Mum, I can't wait!"

"Yes, we hand rear it until it's big enough to return to the wild," Heidi reminded her. "That's where hedgehogs belong."

"It's OK, I won't make a pet of it," Eva promised. "Even though it's really, *really* gorgeous!"

"Good."

"...But," Eva said in what she hoped was a persuasive voice. "While it lives with us, is it OK if I give it a name?"

"Yes, I don't see why not. What are you going to call it?"

The name flashed straight into Eva's mind as she took a quick look around. "Barney – because we found it in a barn!" she told her mum. "Barney the baby hedgehog!"

Chapter Three

"Don't worry – Mum will be here soon," Eva whispered.

Barney had slowly unrolled and set off towards Tom Ingleby's flower beds. He took refuge amongst some bright yellow marigolds.

"I bet you're hungry," she went on. "I wonder what you like to eat."

"Maggots," Tom Ingleby said, appearing at the farmhouse door. "Worms, beetles and slugs."

"Lovely!" Eva grimaced. "I guess we'll stick to cat food."

"Yes, and don't give him cows' milk," Tom advised, leaning against the door with his arms crossed. "People think hedgehogs like a saucer of milk, but it makes them poorly."

As they talked, Eva heard a car in the lane. "See – I said she wouldn't be long!" Eva told Barney, running to meet her mum.

"Here's the carrier," Heidi said, unloading it from the boot of the car. "Now where is the little chap? Let me take a look."

Barney peered out from the flower bed. He twitched his tiny, black nose.

"Oh yes, he's just a baby," Heidi confirmed, crouching down to look at the hedgehog. "Probably about four weeks old."

"He must be really scared," Eva whispered. "I feel so sorry for him."

Her mum nodded. "He definitely wouldn't survive on his own. For a start, he needs to put on weight, and as he probably isn't fully weaned yet that would be hard for him to do. So we'll feed him through a dropper filled with a special glucose preparation," Heidi decided.

Eva set the pet carrier down on the grass whilst Heidi scooped some cat food into a plastic dish. "Let's hope this does the trick."

"Will Barney eat solids?" Eva asked as they stepped back and waited.

Heidi nodded. "He'll already be eating caterpillars and so on, mixed in with his mother's milk."

Eva watched Barney carefully. He'd raised his head and sniffed, but so far he hadn't moved, instead staying hidden amongst the leaves and flowers. "Come on, little Barney!" she urged. "We won't hurt you."

"He's probably in a state of shock," Heidi said slowly. "We might have to pick him up and put him in the carrier."

"Yes, it'll soon be dusk," Tom agreed. "We don't want him to run off now – you'll never find him!"

"But we're not supposed to handle him."
Eva was anxious. "His mother won't want
him if we pick him up!"

Heidi shook her head. "That's true, but I
think we have to face facts, Eva. His
mother isn't coming back for him in
any case."

"You mean, Barney's an orphan?"

"He might just as well be," Heidi agreed.
She went to the car and collected a pair of
thick leather gloves. "From now on this
little hedgehog will be relying on us to
look after him."

"Cool! So can I pick him up?" Eva
stepped forward. "Please, Mum. I was the
one who found him."

Her mother nodded and handed over
the gloves. "Do it gently. I expect he'll curl
up tight."

Eva put on the gloves and knelt down

on the grass. She eased back the broad leaves and slowly cupped her hands around Barney.

The baby hedgehog sensed danger and rolled into a ball.

"Try to get one hand underneath him," Heidi said. "Rock him from side to side then roll him on to your palm. That's it."

Carefully Eva followed her mum's instructions until she had Barney safe between her hands. Then she carried him to the pet carrier and popped him in, rolling him off her palm into the straw-lined box.

"Job done!" Heidi said, quickly closing the mesh door. She picked up the carrier and loaded it into the car. "Thanks, Tom. I hope we haven't been too much of a nuisance," she told him.

The farmer waved them off. "No problem. I'm glad Eva spotted the little fellow."

Eva got in the car and sighed with relief. "Let's go, Mum!" she urged. "Barney must be starving. Animal Magic, here we come!"

"What's wrong with him? He won't unroll." Back at the rescue centre, Karl watched Eva trying to give the baby hedgehog fluid through a plastic dropper. Barney had resisted and stayed curled up tight.

"I can see that for myself." Eva frowned.

"Having trouble?" Jen called across the room. She was nursing a young rabbit called Ozzy who was recovering from surgery on his badly broken leg.

Heidi had been called out on an emergency and had left Eva and Animal Magic's new veterinary assistant, Jen Andrews, to take care of Barney in the small animals unit.

"Yes, how do we get him to unroll?" Eva asked.

"Wait a second while I finish with Ozzy." Quickly, Jen fixed the rabbit's water bottle so that it was within easy reach, then she came across.

"See – Barney's not interested in taking a drink," Eva explained. "He hasn't moved since we brought him in."

Jen ran a hand through her long dark hair. She'd been working at Animal Magic since the middle of the summer, quickly settling in and showing that she knew plenty about small animals in particular. Hamsters were her favourites, closely followed by rabbits. "OK," she told Karl and Eva. "First of all, Karl, I want you to fetch a heat-lamp from the storeroom."

"Coming right up," Karl said, dashing off.

"It'll help restore Barney's body heat," Jen explained.

"What's the reason he won't unroll?" Eva asked. She'd been hoping that the peace and safety of the unit would help him to feel safe.

"Think about it – he's had a bad day," Jen explained, reaching for the leather gloves. "First he loses his mum and brothers and sisters. Second he gets picked up by a giant and taken off to a strange place."

"A *friendly* giant!" Eva insisted.

"But Barney doesn't know that. He's still in a state of shock." Jen put on the gloves and reached into the cage. Gently she rocked Barney back and forth.

"Why are you doing that?" Eva asked.

"The rocking motion calms him down."

"How did you learn all this?"

"When I was a teenager I worked in a hedgehog rescue centre close to where I lived in County Kerry. I learned all sorts of useful tricks. I'll give you their name and you can check out their website."

Gradually, as Jen kept on rocking Barney he began to uncurl.

"Wow, look at that," Karl said when he came back with the lamp.

Eva watched as Barney's head came into view and he peered around with his short-sighted eyes. "Shall I try him with the dropper?" she asked Jen.

"Yes. Hold it above his head and slightly to one side. Try and make the fluid drip into the corner of his mouth."

Eva did exactly as Jen told her, and was

delighted when Barney opened his lips and let the glucose solution dribble into his mouth. "He's drinking it!"

"Well done. Now, Karl, turn the lamp on. I'll fetch the anti-maggot powder. We don't want any unwelcome guests hatching out in the unit, do we?"

"He's cute, isn't he?" Eva asked Karl, feeling a tight knot of worry in her stomach begin to unwind now that little Barney was happily gulping his drink.

Karl nodded. "I'm going to go and email Joel and tell him all about Barney," he decided.

"Yeah, say he should never have left us and gone to work in Russia!" Eva said with a smile. "Oh, and tell him I miss him!"

Chapter Four

Hi, Karl and everyone!

Great to hear from you and I'm glad the good work goes on at Animal Magic. Good on you, Eva the Hedgehog Hero!

Life here is different. Yesterday while you were busy rescuing hedgehogs, I was vaccinating a herd of beef cattle for a farmer who owns several thousand acres of Russian prairie. The wind cuts through you like a knife here.

Still – variety is the spice of life, they say.

Will write more when I get time.

Take care, Joel x

Karl showed Eva the email before he set out on an early morning dog walk with Buddy the golden Labrador-cross. "Hang on, Buddy," he said as the boisterous youngster pulled at his lead. "Do you think Joel likes his new job?" he asked Eva.

"It's hard to tell. But I'm glad it's not me vaccinating hundreds of cattle in the freezing cold." Eva was in a hurry to help Jen in the small animals unit. "Give me hamsters and hedgehogs any day!"

"Morning, Eva!" Jen called, as Eva joined her. Even though it was Sunday and her day off, Jen had come in to check on Ozzy.

"How's Barney?" Eva asked, making a beeline for the baby hedgehog.

She found him snoozing in his cage, half-buried in straw. "I looked at your hedgehog sanctuary website," she told Jen. "It told me lots of stuff I didn't know."

"I'm glad Barney's had a good sleep," Jen commented as she joined Eva. "All these new smells and sounds confuse him. And hedgehogs don't see too well, so that muddles him even more."

"That's what I thought," Eva laughed.

"Barney looks like a little old man who needs new glasses!"

"Anyway, it'll be fine to wake him now that he's had a rest." Jen fetched some scales from a nearby shelf. "Let's weigh him so we can keep a check on his weight gain over this next week or so."

"Cool! Can I do it?" Eva had read how to do this on the website. It meant putting on the thick gloves and rocking Barney on to the palm of her hand, then transferring him gently to the dish of the old-fashioned scales.

"Now put the weights on the other end of the balance until it evens up exactly," Jen told her.

Eva looked anxiously at Barney, whose eyes were open but who was still curled tight in the brass dish. "What if he tries to make a dash for it?"

"He won't. Anyway, we're nearly done," Jen muttered as Eva slid the last disc-shaped weight on to the scales. "He weighs 560 grams."

"Can I take him off now?" Eva checked.

"Yes. Snuggle him back into his straw bed." Jen noted down the figure on a chart she'd set up for Barney. "He needs to reach 600 grams so that he'll be fat enough to get through the winter. The sooner he reaches that weight, the sooner we can let him go. So we need to fatten him up a bit!"

Eva nodded. She put Barney back in his cage and rocked him to and fro until he uncurled. "There, you see – safe and sound."

Rustling deep into the straw, Barney peered out, sniffing hard as Eva dished up some cat food.

"This is for you," she told him. "Yum!"

Barney poked his nose out of the straw. Nervously he shuffled forwards.

"It's scrummy – try it!" Eva whispered.

Sniff-sniff – Barney edged forward. He put his front paws on to the edge of the saucer and dipped his snout into the food. Another quick sniff then he opened his mouth and began to chomp happily.

"Success." Jen smiled. "And I've checked the splint on Ozzy's leg, which seems fine, so I'm out of here!"

Eva nodded. "Enjoy your day off."

"I will. I'm cycling over to Clifton to see some friends. What are you up to?"

Eva checked things off on her fingers. "Feed the rabbits, hamsters and guinea pigs. Take two dogs for walks. Muck out Rosie and Mickey's stables…"

"Stop!" Jen put up both hands. "I'm worn out just thinking about it!"

"Oh, and then this afternoon Annie and I are riding Guinevere." Eva laughed. "That is, if I have time!"

"You should have seen Barney dashing about looking for his mum in Mr Ingleby's yard," Eva told her next door neighbour and best friend, Annie Brooks. Annie was riding Guinevere by the riverbank while Eva walked alongside. "He was so scared he didn't know which way to run."

Annie pulled on the reins as her mum's grey mare stopped to chew grass. "Cut it out, Gwinnie. Mum doesn't like hedgehogs in her garden," she told Eva. "She says they wear a path across her lawn."

"Tut!" Eva swished at the long grass with a stick she'd picked up from the bank. "She ought to love them. They eat the slugs that chomp her lettuce."

"I'll tell her." Annie grinned. Still struggling to raise Gwinnie's head, she slid from the saddle, gave Eva the hard-hat, then handed her the reins. "Your turn!"

Happily, Eva put her foot in the stirrup and sprang into the saddle. "Walk on,

Gwinnie," she said with a click of her tongue.

Guinevere flicked her ears and tossed her long white mane. She set off at a smart walk.

"Trot on!" Eva said with a squeeze of her legs. "Is it OK if I canter?" she asked Annie.

"Go for it!"

Eva turned Guinevere away from the river and sat deep in the saddle, sending the horse into a smooth canter up the hill towards Annie's house. In the distance, Guinevere's foal, Merlin, plus Mickey and Rosie were quietly grazing.

"Whee!" Eva loved the feel of the wind in her face and the thundering sound of the horse's hooves.

Rosie, Merlin and Mickey looked up, then galloped to join in the fun. The little brown and white Shetland soon fell behind the frisky foal and the long-legged donkey, who almost cannoned into Gwinnie and Eva.

"Whoa, Mickey!" Eva yelled, pulling on the reins to bring Gwinnie to a halt.

The donkey bared his teeth and dug in his hooves, coming to a sudden stop beside them.

"Watch where you're going, Mickey!" Eva cried, laughing at stout little Rosie as she trotted up behind Mickey and Merlin.

"It's not fair, is it, Rosie. Everyone has longer legs than you."

Rosie kicked up her heels and put in a little buck of pure joy.

"Hey, Annie, shall we take this lot in from the field and give them a good grooming?" Eva asked, looking over her shoulder to see her friend running up from the riverbank. "I could ride back to the yard and fetch the head collars."

"No need!" Annie's mother's head appeared over the hedge. She must have heard the girls while she'd been working in her garden. "I have head collars here. Wait a minute."

Moments later, Linda appeared with the halters.

"Annie, you lead Mickey and Merlin. Eva, you carry on riding Guinevere back to the yard. I'll bring Rosie along in a few minutes and lend a hand. Then Gwinnie and Merlin can come back into the field overnight. The weather forecast said that it was going to be nice and mild."

"Thanks, Mum." Annie grinned up at Eva. Not so long ago, her mum would have been complaining about the noise made by the animals at the rescue centre, not offering to come and help.

It was the end of a perfect sunny Sunday afternoon in early September, and Eva knew that life didn't get much better than this.

Chapter Five

"Stand still, Mickey!" Annie pleaded with the donkey, brush in hand. "How can I groom you if you keep on prancing about?"

Mickey raised his head and gave an ear-splitting bray.

"Ouch!" In the stable next door, Eva was taking off Guinevere's bridle, ready for her pamper session. "That hurt my ears!"

"That's better." At last Annie managed to corner Mickey. "You want to look smart, don't you? That's it, good boy."

"OK, Merlin, it'll soon be your turn," Eva laughed as the foal nudged her arm, then nuzzled her pocket. "Oh, I see – you want an apple, but those are for later. You'll have to wait until we've finished grooming, before Linda takes you back into your field."

Disappointed, Merlin stuck his head over the stable door and whinnied at Rosie, who was being led across Animal Magic's yard by Linda Brooks.

"Here we are!" Linda sang out. She waved at Mark and Karl.

"Hi, Linda. Nice afternoon!" Mark called from the back door of the old farmhouse.

"Perfect." Linda waited for Mark to join her. "I was wondering – is Heidi around?"

"No, I'm afraid not. Will I do instead?"

Patting Rosie's neck, Linda smiled awkwardly. "No thanks, Mark. It's something I wanted to discuss with Heidi."

Eva listened to the conversation. "What's that about?" she muttered to Annie.

"Search me. Mickey, stand still." Annie thought for a moment. "She probably wants some advice about Gwinnie's teeth. I heard her tell dad she needed the phone number of a good horse dentist."

"You hear that?" Eva asked the grey mare. "You're going to get your teeth filed, you lucky thing!"

Linda brought Rosie over to the stables, and led her into the corner stall.

"If it's a horse dentist you want, I know where Mum keeps the phone numbers," Eva offered, brushing away at Gwinnie's mane until it shone.

Linda shook her head. "Actually, that wasn't what I wanted to talk to Heidi about."

"Steady!" Annie warned Mickey as he stomped his feet. She leaned out of the donkey's stable. "Mum, what's the mystery?

You're blushing! What's going on?"

"Nothing," Linda said quietly.

"Yes, it is!" Annie knew her mum only too well. She left Mickey to fidget and went over. "Come on, Mum. What are you up to?"

"Not now, Annie. Let me talk to Heidi first." With a shake of her head, Linda bolted Rosie's door.

The little Shetland went straight to her hay-net and began to eat. *Munch-munch* – her strong teeth ground away at the sweet hay.

"Mum, tell me!" Annie insisted. Suddenly a glint came into her eye. "If it isn't about Gwinnie, is it Merlin?"

"No. Don't pester me." With her back turned, Linda set about brushing Rosie.

"Or Rosie?" Annie said, sounding excited.

Eva could sense something important in

the air. She stopped grooming Gwinnie and waited to hear more.

Annie wouldn't let her mum off the hook. "It *is* – it's Rosie, isn't it?"

Linda sighed. She crouched down and put her arm around the sturdy little Shetland's neck. "Oh all right, I give in. I'll tell you girls what you want to know."

Eva and Annie nodded eagerly.

"I've developed a real soft spot for this young lady," Linda confessed. "And I think she likes me."

Rosie turned her head and nuzzled Linda's cheek.

Annie and Eva held their breath.

"So, I've decided to ask Heidi if she'll let me adopt Rosie!" Linda announced. "I want her to come and live with us permanently!"

"So we broke out the apples and celebrated!" Eva told Heidi and Jen later that afternoon. "Of course we gave Rosie the biggest and juiciest one."

"It's fantastic news," Heidi agreed. "Annie must have been so pleased."

"Yes, *well* excited." Eva watched as her mum lifted the patient on to the surgery table. It was a stray dog, painfully thin, which Jen had discovered trapped in an empty lock-up garage in town. She'd phoned Mark and he'd driven into town and brought the stray back to Animal Magic.

"From what we can gather, it seems like someone dumped the poor thing in a garage and locked the door." Heidi listened to the dog's heartbeat, then examined her eyes and mouth.

"She's dehydrated and she only weighs about half of what would be her normal weight, but given time and some TLC she should be OK."

Eva sighed as the smooth-haired white dog tried to raise her head, then let it loll back on the table. "I'll get Karl to take a picture. Do you know where he is?"

"In the small animals unit, the last I knew."

Quickly Eva went to find her brother, but he wasn't where she expected him to be. The unit was all quiet and Eva found herself drawn to Barney's cage. She peered in to see how her little friend was doing. "And how are you? Are you hungry? Shall I give you some food?"

For once Barney didn't curl into a ball at the sound of Eva's approach. Instead he shuffled to the wire mesh door and snuffled in his short-sighted way.

"Yes, it's me," Eva whispered. "I'm the one who feeds you, remember!"

Little Barney poked his long nose through the mesh while Eva prepared his food. When she opened the door he stuck his nose straight into the dish.

"Better than beetles and toads, huh?" Eva grinned. Like Eva, Karl had been on the hedgehog website and discovered all about their diet. He'd told Eva that morning over breakfast.

"Maggots, worms, insects, beetles, earwigs, slugs, caterpillars, toads and dead mice!" he'd announced, making Eva spit out her cornflakes.

Barney looked too cute to have dead mice on his menu. But then, as Heidi had pointed out, hedgehogs probably turned their noses up at human treats like cream cakes and chocolate cookies.

In any case, Barney was tucking in to his cat food, happily piling on the pounds.

Or grams, Eva thought. Then she got to thinking about Barney's family. *I wonder how many brothers and sisters you've got. And if your mum misses you. Or if she'll come back to Mr Ingleby's farm to look for you, in spite of what Mum thinks.*

Ignoring her, Barney guzzled his way through his supper.

"OK, so your mum might reject you because we've handled you and left our scent. And I'm totally cool with hand-rearing you because you're gorgeous. But that's not the point..."

Suddenly Karl burst in with a huge grin on his face. "Smidge and Smudge have been adopted by the Scaife family. They seemed really nice."

"Cool." Eva pretended she hadn't been deep in conversation with Barney. "Can you go into the surgery and photograph a new stray dog?" she asked.

Karl nodded. "So what's not the point?" he asked, picking up from where Eva had left off with Barney. "It's OK, you can drop the act. I heard you doing your Doctor Doolittle talking to the animals thing!"

Eva tutted. "I just thought – what if Barney isn't the only baby hedgehog who got lost in Mr Ingleby's barn? What if he's got brothers and sisters?"

"And no mum?" Karl nodded slowly. "It's possible."

"More than possible!" Eva insisted. "I checked the website and it says there are usually three or four babies in one litter. They're called hoglets! Isn't that cute?"

Karl rolled his eyes. "Cute? I hope you're

not getting too attached, Eva. And remember – you're only guessing that the mum isn't still around." Karl was being logical as usual.

"I know." Eva bit her lip. "But what *if*?"

"OK, say you're right," Karl argued, walking out of the unit with Eva following. "Say there are more orphan babies out there. What do you plan to do about it?"

"I don't know yet. I'm going to carry on thinking," she replied, closing the door behind her. "But, Karl, I'll tell you one thing for sure – I'm not going to forget about it!"

Chapter Six

"So I was wondering, Annie, if you'd like to camp out in Mr Ingleby's barn?"

Annie stood at the front door, her mouth gaping open in surprise. "Just run through that again," she begged Eva. "You want to find out if there are any more baby hedgehogs like Barney, and the way you plan to do it is to have a sleepover in the barn at High Trees Farm. Did I get that right?"

Eagerly Eva nodded. The idea had come to her at teatime. In a second she'd jumped up and started to organize.

"Uh-oh, Eva's just had one of her eureka moments!" Mark had laughed.

"More hoglets ... probably lost ... camp out ... Annie!" she'd gabbled.

In the end, her mum and dad had agreed to the barn sleepover, but only as long as Linda let Annie go along too, and provided Tom Ingleby didn't mind.

"But don't be disappointed if no other hoglets show up," Heidi had warned. "You two could be out there all night and see absolutely nothing!"

"Mad!" Karl had said, retreating to his computer. "I'm going to email Joel and tell him that my sister is as nutty as a fruitcake!"

Eva had gone ahead anyway and dug

out her sleeping bag, a fleece and a thick pair of socks. Now she was at Annie's door, desperate to get on with her plan.

"Quick – ask your mum!" she urged Annie. "Remind her we're still on summer holidays, so there's no school tomorrow. Promise her we'll be careful, and say Mr and Mrs Ingleby will keep an eye on us."

"I heard all that," Linda said, coming out from the lounge. Luckily, she was still in a good mood over Rosie. In fact, she'd been busily looking through a Build-Your-Own-Stable catalogue when Eva had knocked at the door. "So, Eva – this is Operation Baby Hedgehog, is it?"

Eva nodded. "Can Annie sleep out with me, please?"

"If she wants to – yes, she can."

"Of course you want to, don't you?" Eva didn't give Annie chance to object.

"You need to pack a sleeping bag and a bottle of water, plus snacks…"

"Whoa!" Annie cut Eva off mid-flow. She stood in her flowery top with cut-off white trousers and smart new trainers. "Do I look as if I'm dressed to sleep out in a mucky old barn?"

"Oh!" Eva's face fell. "Are you saying you don't want to?"

For a split second Annie kept Eva in suspense. Then she broke out in a wide grin. "Course I do! Give me five minutes to change, and I'll be round at your place."

Eva breathed a sigh of relief. "So not funny," she muttered, scooting back to Animal Magic, where she made a couple of doorstep cheese sandwiches and packed them in her school rucksack.

"Apples?" Mark suggested, putting them in the bag for her. "Flapjacks? And by the way, your mum rang Tom Ingleby and he says it's OK to do your sleepover there."

Soon Eva was packed and ready, her bag stuffed with goodies, plus two strong torches with new batteries and a pair of thick gloves just in case.

"Here comes Annie now," Heidi said, looking through the window. "Your dad is going to drive you over to High Trees." Giving Eva a quick hug, she saw her on her way. "I've put a pet carrier and a tin of cat food in the back of the van," she reminded her. "And remember – don't handle any hedgehogs without gloves – those prickles are sharp!"

"Bye, Mum!" Eva called. "Bye, Mickey!" she yelled as the donkey brayed from his stable. "Bye, Karl!" She waved at her brother sitting by his bedroom window. "Take care of Barney for me. Tell him I'll see him tomorrow!"

"I hope you don't mind – we've made a den in the barn," Eva told Mrs Ingleby, who was just back from her early evening church service. Eva's dad had already gone into the house to chat with Tom.

As soon as Annie and Eva had arrived at the farm, they'd started shifting bales of straw to build a shelter from the wind that blew through the open-sided barn. Then they'd laid out the pet carrier and cat food, plus their sleeping bags and other belongings.

Mrs Ingleby smiled. "I hope you'll be nice and cosy in there. If you need anything, just knock at our door."

Eva thanked her then went with Annie to check out the view from their den.

"We can see the whole farmyard from here," Annie confirmed. "And a bit of the lane, plus that jumble of stones and the cement mixer over there..."

"That's where the Inglebys are building a new house for Adam." Eva climbed to the top of the stack to look round the back of the barn. "Just trees, fields and hedges," she reported, sliding back down. "Hey, this is exciting, isn't it?"

Annie nodded. "Better than camping."

"Better than anything!" Eva insisted, nestling into the straw den. And the best thing of all was that they were out to rescue more baby hedgehogs!

"What was that noise?" Annie gasped.

It was eleven o'clock and the farmyard was pitch black.

"An owl," Eva told her. "Nothing to worry about."

Annie sat huddled in her sleeping bag. "What was that?" she asked again.

"What? Where?"

"Down there – something moved!"

"Probably a mouse."

"Or a rat!" Annie sounded scared. Sleeping out was turning into a nightmare of eerie hoots, beating wings, soft shuffles and quick scurries.

"I'm sure it's not!" Eva insisted, though her own nerves were a bit on edge. It was so dark! Clouds hid the moon. The world lay in deep shadow.

"We haven't even seen a sign of any hedgehogs," Annie complained. "And we've been here for hours!"

"Wait a bit longer. The lights in the house have only just gone off. Now's the time when everything comes out of hiding."

"Such as?" Annie asked, her voice quavering.

"Such as badgers," Eva replied. "And foxes. Owls. Bats. Hedgehogs." She shone her torch out across the farmyard and spotted Missie disappearing through the cat flap into the farmhouse. Then she saw another creature – something the size of a big dog, with a long nose and bushy tail. "Fox!" she whispered, aiming the torch.

The fox turned to stare up into the beam of light. His yellow eyes flashed.

"Spooky!" Annie whispered.

The fox flicked the white tip of his tail and loped off down the lane, out of sight.

Just then Eva spotted something else that deserved a closer look – small movements in the Inglebys' flower border, and when she listened closely, the high, piping sound of animals in distress. "Annie, listen – this could be it!"

Annie flicked on her own torch. Two beams raked the flower bed. The high cries came to a sudden stop.

"I'm going to take a closer look," Eva decided, getting up and creeping forwards.

Annie didn't want to be left alone. "Wait, I'm coming too!" she hissed.

Soon the two girls stood at the barn entrance, deciding on their next move.

"Let's switch off the torches," Eva suggested. "If there are baby hedgehogs hiding among the plants, they won't come out if we leave them on."

With the flick of two switches, the girls were pitched into total darkness.

"It's giving me goosebumps!" Annie whispered. The wind blew across the fields and through the tall ash trees behind the barn.

Eva waited for her eyes to get used to the dark. Gradually, she made out the shape of the farmhouse across the yard, and then an animal coming around the corner. Maybe it was Missie out on the prowl after mice again, or perhaps something bigger and more dangerous...

"The fox is back!" Annie gasped. She too had seen the intruder.

The fox crept towards the flower border, ignoring Eva and Annie. He seemed to have his mind fixed on something else, head low and sniffing the ground. He was following a trail!

"Oh no you don't!" Eva muttered. She flashed on her torch and dashed forward, just as the fox pounced and three baby hedgehogs broke cover and ran in all directions across Tom Ingleby's yard.

Chapter Seven

"Back off!" Eva shone her torch straight at the fox.

He curled his top lip and snarled back at her.

"Go on, scoot!" Eva insisted. "Annie, you try to round up the hoglets while I deal with the fox."

Anxiously, Annie ran after the first baby hedgehog, who had taken cover inside the barn. Quickly, she put on the gloves and clumsily scooped the hedgehog between her palms.

Meanwhile, the fox turned from the beam of light and slowly slunk away.

Her heart beating fast, Eva watched him vanish down the lane. "Thank goodness!" she muttered. The fox's teeth had looked sharp and nasty.

"I've caught one of the babies!" Annie called from the barn.

"Great. Put him in the carrier. Did you see which way the other two went?"

"One ran towards the house."

Quickly, Eva began to search the flower bed where they'd found Barney. She used her torch to peer under the leaves. "I know this light is scary," she murmured. "But don't be frightened. We're here to help."

"Any luck?" Annie had put the first baby in the carrier and joined Eva.

"Not yet." Eva was surprised how fast

the hoglets had run. She had a sinking feeling that they would never find the two who were still on the loose.

Suddenly, Annie heard a scuffling sound behind one of Mrs Ingleby's marigold pots by the farmhouse door. She shone her torch and discovered the second cowering baby. "Over here!" she hissed.

"Cool, Annie!" Eva heaved a sigh of relief. "Can you manage here while I track down the last one?"

"Go ahead. Did you see any sign of the mother?"

Eva shook her head. "She's definitely not around. If she was, she'd have been here with them when the fox showed up."

"Do you think it means she's dead?" Gently, Annie rolled the second hoglet on to her gloved palm.

"Yes. Which means I need to find hoglet number three – right away!"

But where to start? Eva shone the torch around the farmyard, trying to remember how the three babies had scattered – one towards the barn, one towards the house and – yes, that was right – one had sprinted for the building site at the side of the barn. Eva set off after this last one.

She shone the torch over the pile of bricks and stones, and over the dusty orange cement mixer. The builders had made a start on digging the foundations, so she had to jump across a pile of earth and a narrow trench. No – that couldn't be right – the baby wouldn't have been able to cross the trench. Eva retraced her steps and kept on searching.

This is hopeless! she thought. *Like looking for a needle in a haystack.*

But the idea of the lonely orphan drove her on. Her feet crunched over gravel as she shone her torch amongst the rubble, then over the neat stack of bricks.

Eeee-ee! A tiny cry stopped Eva in her tracks. *Eeee!*

It came from an untidy coil of green hose attached to a tap on the side of the barn. Eva turned off the torch and tiptoed across.

The noise stopped. Had she imagined it? Carefully she crouched by the hose.

Eee-eee! came the helpless, lonely cry.

Eva held her breath and waited. There was a small movement, another high-pitched cry, and then the baby emerged from the curled hose.

Yes! On the spur of the moment, Eva took off her fleece jacket and used it to pick up the hedgehog. She ran to the barn door and showed it to Annie. "Let's put it in with the other two," she gasped.

The two captured hedgehogs squeaked and cried as Annie opened the door. Quickly, Eva lowered the third wanderer into the carrier. "Success!" she said, breathing a sigh of relief.

"You're safe now!" Eva promised. Safe from the fox. Protected from the dangers of the big wide world.

After the excitement of the round-up, silence had fallen. Apart from the wind blowing through the ash trees, there was no sound.

"Look at them tucking in to that dish of food!" Annie murmured.

The two girls were snuggled in their sleeping bags, watching the hoglets feed.

"Barney will be really pleased to see you." Eva sighed. "And when we get you back we can weigh you and dust you with maggot powder, and feed you up and then..."

"Then what?" Annie interrupted as Eva slowed down.

"Then they'll be ready for the winter," Eva faltered.

"How do you mean – ready?"

"Ready to be released back into the wild," Eva explained.

As the three tiny babies munched greedily, she glanced up at her friend and sighed. "That's the way it works, Annie. We can't turn them into pets. They're wild creatures. That's where they belong."

It was after midnight before Eva and Annie fell asleep. The farmyard was still. An owl flitted into the barn and perched in the rafters.

At dawn a pink sky woke the girls and the first thing they did was check the hoglets.

"One – two – three," Annie counted three little heads peeping out of the bed of newspaper and straw. Three pointed snouts and three pairs of furry ears.

"Breakfast time!" Eva announced, spooning food into their dish.

The babies gulped and guzzled, snorted and sniffed.

"Cute!" Annie cooed over them. "How about calling this one with the fluffy eyebrows Tufty?"

"And this one Patch?" Eva recognized the baby they'd found in the flower bed by a small bare patch on its back. "And the one who legged it towards the building site can be Scooby."

"Tufty, Patch and Scooby!" Annie agreed happily.

"Not that we're turning them into pets!" Eva added hurriedly.

They both laughed and rolled up their sleeping bags, waiting for the sound of the Animal Magic van to come up the lane.

Chapter Eight

"Mission accomplished!" Jen said when she drove into the farmyard. "One look at your two faces tells me that the plan was a great success."

Eva and Annie beamed and nodded. "Come and see!" Annie said.

Jen peered through the mesh front of the carrier and counted the babies. "No mother?" she checked.

"No." Eva shook her head. "You know that hedgehogs have a run which they use every night?" she said to Jen. "Well, what happens if the run gets blocked – by a flood, say, or by something man-made, like a new house getting built?"

"Then they get totally lost and confused," Jen replied, picking up on Eva's train of thought. "You're talking about the building site round the corner here?"

Eva nodded. "Scooby – this one with the black legs – made a dash straight down there, only there was a trench stopping him from going the way he might usually have run, before they started digging."

Jen decided to take a look. Leading Annie and Eva across the building site, she opened a gate and gazed down the sloping field.

"What are we looking for?" Annie asked.

"See if you can spot a track worn in the grass and the undergrowth – especially by the hedges."

"Like this?" Eva asked. She pointed to a narrow track running alongside the hedge and across through the trees towards the back of the Inglebys' barn.

"Exactly!" Jen cried. "And look – the track cuts by the barn, under the gate and comes to a stop right against the stack of bricks and rubble."

"It's Barney's run!" Eva gasped. "And it's just like I thought – it's been cut off by the builders. No wonder the hoglets got lost!"

"Ace detective Eva strikes again!" Annie grinned. "I bet you're right – and it explains a lot."

"Except what happened to their mum," Jen said slowly. "And I guess that's something we may never know. Let's get those babies back to Animal Magic," she said briskly, heading back towards the van. "Heidi's expecting us. There are a thousand and one jobs to do."

Back in the small animals unit, Eva was telling her mum the whole story about the hedgehog run and the building site. "But the hedgehogs were there first!" she complained.

Annie had been dragged off by her mum to have breakfast and get a shower while Eva and Jen reunited Scooby, Patch and Tufty with Barney.

Now Heidi was casting an eye over the three new arrivals.

"I'm sure Tom and Adam Ingleby didn't know they were building over a hedgehog run," Eva's mum pointed out. "They wouldn't do it on purpose. It's just an unfortunate accident."

"It makes no difference." Eva sighed. "Anyway, they know now because Adam came out to talk to us before we drove away."

"And you told him?" Heidi guessed.

"In no uncertain terms," Jen said wryly. "As I remember it, Eva's exact words to Adam were, 'Did you know that you're building a house over a hedgehog run?'"

"Yes. And Adam said he was sorry but it was done now. The builders had started work on the foundations and there was no way he could alter it." Eva frowned as she told her mum about the discussion.

"Which is true." Cool and calm as usual, Heidi went to check Ozzy's leg.

"I said the builders could have left a passageway down the side of the barn for the hedgehogs to keep on using," Eva went on. She stayed by the hoglets' cage and watched Barney sniff then greet Scooby while Patch and Tufty rummaged in the straw. "Adam said they could have if they'd known, but it was too late now."

"Which it is," Heidi said quietly. "I hope you weren't rude to Adam, Eva. After all, the Inglebys did let you camp out in their barn."

"Not rude, but firm," Jen said. "And I must admit, I'm with Eva on this."

Eva glanced eagerly across the room. "And Jen agreed with me that it's still worthwhile asking the Inglebys to clear a passage down the side of the barn. I had the idea when we were in the van, coming home. I was thinking ahead."

"OK," Heidi said slowly. Satisfied with the rabbit's progress, she put him back in his cage. "In what way, thinking ahead?"

"Like this!" Eva explained. "The builders clear a passageway for wild animals, including hedgehogs, to come and go. They build a fence to block off the building work. Then we make nest boxes for Barney, Tufty, Scooby and Patch. We put them amongst the ash trees at the back of the barn."

"Which we have to do anyway," Jen pointed out. "Build nest boxes, I mean."

Heidi nodded. "Yes, I know. It would be the way we'd reintroduce the hedgehogs back into the wild – by giving them a safe nest to take refuge in."

"And if we put them near to High Trees Farm, Barney and the others would recognize where they were and they'd soon find the new passageway which the builders would have made for them!" By now Eva was bubbling over with excitement. "What do you think, Mum?"

Heidi pursed her lips. "I'm not sure. It's a lot to ask. Then again, builders are meant to be sympathetic to wildlife these days."

"And the Wildlife Trust is very hot on the issue," Jen agreed. "Especially when a species is under threat, which hedgehogs are."

Heidi sighed. "I'm not arguing with that. I'm just saying that Animal Magic has to stay on good terms with its neighbours. We can't march in and make demands, asking Tom Ingleby to spend more money than he already is on this house for Adam."

"But if we ask nicely…" Eva begged. "And if we told him that one hedgehog –

the hoglets' mum – has already died because they blocked the run…"

"No, we can't say that," Heidi insisted. "We have to be certain of our facts, and we're never going to know that for sure."

"OK. But if we say Dad, Karl and I will help build the fence, and it won't cost much…" Eva gave her mum a pleading look. "Please let me ask Mr Ingleby," she begged. "Please, Mum – please!"

Chapter Nine

"You're doing well with those baby hedgehogs," Mark told Eva at lunchtime the next day. He had a day off work and was spending it helping Heidi with paperwork. Now he was taking a break, watching Eva weigh the hoglets.

"Tell Mum that," Eva replied, placing Patch on the scales. She was still on tenterhooks, waiting for a solution to the hedgehog-versus-house debate.

"Tell me what?" Heidi asked, popping

her head around the door.

"Eva's a natural with these hedgehogs," Mark repeated. "Look how expertly she handles them."

"565 grams." Eva noted Patch's weight on a chart, then went on to weigh Scooby. "Jen taught me how to do this," she told her dad.

"Oh yes, I've just seen Jen," Heidi said, coming in properly. She closed the door behind her. "She showed me a design for nest boxes and said she's happy to make two for this little family in her spare time."

"586 grams. Little fatty." Eva recorded Scooby's weight and popped him back in his cage. "Did she mention the fence at High Trees?" she asked hopefully.

"Ah yes – the fence *you're* going to put up, apparently," Heidi said, turning to Mark. "With Karl's help."

"I am?" he asked. "What fence is this?"

It was Eva's cue. She rushed in with her explanation: "Hedgehog run ... builders' trench ... Adam's house ... but the hedgehogs were there first!"

Mark listened carefully. He looked at Eva's eager face, then at Heidi. "So Karl and I have to build a fence to restore the hedgehog run, is that it?"

"If Mum agrees," Eva cut in, looking from one to the other, willing her dad to be on her side. Inside the cage, Patch and Scooby were play-fighting with Barney and Tufty, scampering amongst the clean straw.

At last her dad spoke. "That sounds like a brilliant idea, Eva."

"It does?" Eva's face lit up. Now it was all down to her mum.

"I think if we ask Tom Ingleby in the right way, he won't say no," Mark said.

"In the *right* way!" Heidi insisted. "So that we still get on with our neighbours."

"But we can ask?" Eva pleaded with her mum. *"Please, please, please!"*

Heidi nodded. "I'm outvoted three to one," she acknowledged. "Go on – go ahead and build your fence. Put those babies back where they belong!"

Early that evening Mark took Eva to High Trees Farm. "Stay calm," he told her. "Remember your manners, and if the Inglebys say no to the fence, you have to accept it with good grace."

"OK," Eva promised, getting out of the van. All afternoon she'd been rehearsing her speech.

"Hello, Mark. Hello, Eva." Mrs Ingleby was at the front door watering her plants. "How are you doing with those little hedgehogs?"

"Great, thank you," Eva replied. "Actually, that's what we've come to talk to you and

Mr Ingleby and Adam about." *Stay calm. Be polite.* Her heart was racing.

Mrs Ingleby put down her watering can. "You don't think there are any more babies to rescue, do you?"

"No. It's about Adam's house."

The farmer's wife tilted her head to one side. "Oh yes. Adam mentioned the hedgehog run. I'm sorry we didn't realize what we were doing. I know you must be upset."

"Who's upset?" Tom Ingleby asked, appearing at the door in his slippers. "What is it, Eva? Did something happen to the hoglets?"

Eva felt a nudge from her dad, so she cleared her throat and began her speech. "No, the babies are fine, thanks, Mr Ingleby. Jen is making nest boxes for them so we can release them back into the wild."

"And?" the farmer prompted. He could see that Eva was nervous.

"And we'd like to bring them back here, if that's OK with you. Plus, I've had an idea that would help them find their way around." Now that she'd started, Eva rushed on at full speed. Even when Mrs Ingleby looked surprised and Tom Ingleby shook his head, she gabbled on.

"A fence? You'll build it? It won't cost us anything?" Mr Ingleby repeated, as if he couldn't believe what he'd just heard.

"Please say yes," Eva said. "We wouldn't make a mess and we wouldn't get in the way. We'd build the fence in the evenings, after the builders have gone."

"And you think it would work?" Mrs Ingleby asked, anxiously. "Would the hedgehogs use the run if you gave it back to them?"

Eva took a deep breath. OK, she hadn't stayed calm, but she'd definitely been polite. "We don't know for sure, but we hope so."

There was a silence which seemed to last for ever.

"Your girl has a lot of spirit, I'll say that for her," Tom said to Mark at last.

It was Mrs Ingleby who gave the verdict. "Go right ahead and build your fence, Eva. And I'll keep my fingers crossed that it works!"

"All hands on deck!" Mark cried as they set to work next evening.

Mark, Heidi, Karl, Eva and Annie had driven to High Trees with timber posts and all the tools they needed.

"Fence posts have to be two metres

apart. Measure them out. Dig holes a metre deep."

Out came the orders from Mark. The others got busy.

"Why do the posts have to go so deep?" Annie wondered.

"To stop them blowing over. It's windy up here," Mark explained. "Karl and Eva, you mark these flat planks into two metre lengths. Or just a couple of centimetres over. We'll saw the planks and hammer them horizontally into the upright posts. Here's the measuring tape. Get cracking with that."

"You hold steady, and I'll mark with the felt-tip," Karl said quickly. There were no arguments, just heads down and getting on as fast as they could. By sunset, eight fence posts stood tall and firm in the ground.

It was then that Adam Ingleby drove up the lane and got out of his car. "Can I make myself useful?" he asked. "We've got some spare timber stacked away in the barn. Maybe you can make use of it."

"For sure!" Eva grabbed at the offer with both hands. "Show us where it is before it gets dark."

Chapter Ten

"600 grams exactly!"

Barney sat on the scales peering up at Eva. He was plump and healthy, ready for a spot of adventure.

"No, don't do that!" Eva said as she saw him poke his nose over the edge of the brass dish. She put her gloved hand out just in time to stop him from leaping on to the counter below.

"Whoa, well caught!" Jen called as she came in. "Do you need any help?"

"No thanks." Carefully, Eva put the lively hedgehog back in his cage. "Barney weighs 600 grams. That means he's ready!"

"Yes, but we're not." All week Jen had been making the nest boxes. She'd finished one – a wooden box 50 centimetres square, but still had to construct the entrance tunnel for the second. Meanwhile, Mark's team had built the fence.

"We have to go back to the farm tonight to finish the run," Eva told her. "It should be done by tomorrow, which is Sunday, so the builders won't be there."

"Likewise I need one more session on the boxes." Jen seemed pleased that their plans were coming together. "Shall we say tomorrow for a definite release date?"

Eva nodded, but she felt her heart sink.

Tomorrow? That was soon. Somehow it took her by surprise.

"I know – it's tough," Jen said, looking at Eva's face. "You can't help getting attached, no matter how hard you try."

"I'm worried," Eva confessed. "I hope the hoglets are all going to be OK." She pictured Barney back at High Trees. He was getting too cheeky by half – the type to act without thinking. Scooby too would dash at things, while Patch and Tufty would probably follow where the others led.

"It's the fox," she explained. "And badgers, if there are any, which there's bound to be."

"Which is why I make entrance tunnels too small for badgers and foxes to squeeze through," Jen reminded her. "And remember – hedgehogs have a brilliant self-defence system which they carry around on their backs."

"Their prickles," Eva nodded, still not convinced.

"So let's have a trial run tonight, before we go up to High Trees," Jen suggested. "You go next door and ask Annie's mum if we can use her lawn. And while you're doing that, I'll get to work and finish the nest boxes."

Exactly a week after Eva had found Barney lost and alone, she and Annie had their second session camping out.

This time it was in Annie's garden, and they had strict instructions from Linda Brooks.

"No trampling on my flower beds. No leaving the garden under any circumstances!"

"We promise!" the girls chorused.

So, with torches and gloves at the ready, safe inside their two-man tent, they kept watch on the two hedgehog nest boxes placed carefully in the middle of Linda's lawn.

"I hope the hoglets aren't too scared to come out," Annie whispered.

"Me too," Eva agreed. "And I hope we haven't handled them too much – made them too tame." It was Eva's worst worry that Barney, Patch, Scooby and Tufty wouldn't be able to fend for themselves.

A full moon shone brightly. There was no wind. Everything was silent.

"Look!" Eva whispered. She pointed to the nearest box.

A small, pointed nose had appeared at the end of the tunnel, then a head and eventually a round, prickly body.

Annie held her hand to her lips as Barney emerged, soon followed by Patch. She and Eva watched the two hoglets sniff the grass then quickly pick up the scent of fresh cat food left in a dish at the edge of the lawn. They scuttled across and began to guzzle.

"Here comes Scooby!" Eva murmured.

"Ssshhh!" Annie warned.

Scooby and then Tufty joined Barney and Patch and tucked in.

Hardly able to keep quiet, Eva gave Annie a thumbs up. So far so good. But what would happen when the hoglets had gobbled up all the food?

Go for a wander, as hedgehogs do – that was the answer. Eva gripped her torch and prayed that Barney wouldn't lead the others too far from the boxes.

He went to Linda's rose bed and snuffled around while the others zig-zagged here and there. He dug a little hole and found a worm. *Yum!*

Come back! Eva pleaded silently as he ventured off towards the hedge.

Suddenly, from the stables next door, there was a mighty eee-*aawww*!

"Ouch, Mickey!" Annie yelped.

His bray split the silence and sent the hoglets scurrying back across the lawn into their nest boxes. First Barney, then

Patch sprinted safely down their tunnel. Then Scooby and Tufty vanished from sight.

"Cool!" Eva and Annie cried. Eva gave Annie a high-five. Better than so-far-so-good, their plan for the baby hedgehogs was working perfectly!

Chapter Eleven

The fence was built. The hedgehog run was covered with a woodchip mulch. Mark and the team had planted a few bushes and Eva had collected worms from Annie's garden in preparation for the big event.

"You've done all you can," Heidi told her on Sunday evening.

Eva and Jen had just spent an hour with Barney and the others. Eva had given them one last feed, then relined the nest boxes with fresh straw before she put the young hedgehogs back in. Now it was time to go.

"Don't feel too sad," Jen murmured to Eva as they carried the babies out to Mark's van. "You've done such a good job on this, believe me."

Eva's lip trembled. "I can't help feeling sad. I'm going to miss them so much. Especially Barney."

"I know – but..."

Eva nodded. "...But they belong up at High Trees. I do know that – honestly!"

Mark, Jen and Eva drove in the van. Heidi took Karl and Annie in the car. It was dusk. The Inglebys were waiting by the barn to greet them.

"Operation Hedgehog successfully

completed!" Tom Ingleby smiled as Eva and Annie carried the nest boxes down the new passageway, and placed them amongst the ash trees behind the barn.

"Quick as you can – it's growing dark," Mrs Ingleby encouraged.

"OK, but wait a sec." Eva ran back to the van and brought out her jar of wriggling worms. She scattered them amongst the layer of woodchip in the run. "Ready!" she called, joining the others.

"Stand well back!" Adam said, taking the group downwind of the nest boxes.

It was a long wait, but it was worth it – everyone agreed.

They waited until the owl flew from the treetop into the barn, until the bats had flitted out of the rafters to catch the last insects of the day.

All was quiet under the ash trees.

Then it happened. In the dim half-light a hoglet poked his nose out of his box.

Barney! Eva recognized her favourite in a flash.

Barney the adventurer, big and strong, bravely leading the way. He snorted, as if telling the others it was safe to come out. Soon all four hedgehogs were happily snuffling and poking about in amongst the undergrowth.

Eva grinned at Annie. "So sweet!" she mouthed.

And confident, doing what hedgehogs do. Brave Barney was the first to find his way to the new run, of course.

Eva held her breath. He was sniffing and scampering on a zigzag track, smelling worms! Nose to the ground, he stepped on to the woodchip, calling for the others to follow. *Eee-ee-ee!* One step, two and then three – further down the run, finding his first worm, gobbling it up!

"I'm so happy I could cry!" Eva whispered through trembling lips.

"Time to go," Heidi said, putting her arm around Eva's shoulder. "Barney is going to be just fine, thanks to you."

"And Jen," Eva reminded her. She took one last look over her shoulder as they crossed the farmyard. "And Annie, and Dad and everyone! Thanks to us all, Barney is back where he belongs!"

Collect all the books in the series!

Honey
The unwanted puppy

Charlie
The home-alone kitten

Merlin
The homeless foal

Rusty
The injured fox cub

Bella
The runaway rabbit

Dilly
The lost duckling

Harry
The abandoned hamster

Barney
The baby hedgehog

Visit the Animal Magic website:
www.animalmagicrescue.net

And look out for Animal Rescue's Christmas title!

The doorstep puppy

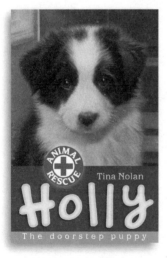

When Holly, a gorgeous Border collie puppy, runs away from home and turns up at Animal Magic on Christmas Eve, half-starved and shivering, Eva falls in love instantly. It proves easy to track down Holly's owners and the rescue centre arranges to return her on Christmas Day. But Eva's determined to investigate why Holly ran away in the first place...

And watch out for
the following book
in the series!

The perfect pony